DINO-DANCING

Lisa Wheeler
Illustrations by Barry Gott

CAROLRHODA BOOKS MINNEAPOLIS

**To Jan's Dance Connection in Brooklyn, MI.
Thanks for your help! —L.W.**

To Rose, Finn, and Nandi —B.G.

Carolrhoda Books
A division of Lerner Publishing Group, Inc.
241 First Avenue North
Minneapolis, MN 55401 USA

For reading levels and more information, look up this title at
www.lernerbooks.com.

Designed by Kimberly Morales.
Main body text set in Churchward Samoa 22/36.
Typeface provided by Chank.
The illustrations in this book were created in Adobe Illustrator
and Photoshop and Corel Painter.

Library of Congress Cataloging-in-Publication Data

Names: Wheeler, Lisa, 1963- author. | Gott, Barry, illustrator.
Title: Dino-dancing / Lisa Wheeler ; illustrations by Barry Gott.
Description: Minneapolis : Carolrhoda Books, [2017] | Summary: "Dinosaurs
   compete in genres of dance from hip-hop to ballet to swing dancing and
   more at the Dino-Dancing Finale"— Provided by publisher.
Identifiers: LCCN 2016042759 (print) | LCCN 2017011592 (ebook) | ISBN
   9781512448542 (eb pdf) | ISBN 9781512403169 (lb : alk. paper)
Subjects: | CYAC: Stories in rhyme. | Dinosaurs—Fiction. | Dance—Fiction.
   | Contests—Fiction.
Classification: LCC PZ8.3.W5668 (ebook) | LCC PZ8.3.W5668 Dgm 2017
   (print) | DDC [E]—dc23

LC record available at https://lccn.loc.gov/2016042759

Manufactured in the United States of America
1-39167-21081-3/7/2017

The Paleo Theater sparkles bright.
DINO-DANCING FINALE TONIGHT!

PALEO

In sequins, tights, or baggy pants,
the dinosaurs are ready to dance!

Nervous dinos scan the crowd.

They hope to make their families proud.

Troodon's Dance Crew fans turn out!

"Go, TDC!" the Red crowds shout.

Herbivores in the center section
cheer for **Minmi's Dance Connection**!

Just minutes till the curtains rise.
Dinos stretch their tails and thighs.

They flex their feet and twist their waists,
costumes ready, shoes are laced.

Cue the curtains! Spotlight's bright.
A large ballerina steps into the light.

Allosaurus is up on her toes:
Scarlet tutu, crimson hose.

Plié, jeté and arabesque,
Pirouette! Pirouette! Pirouette!
Rest.

Beautiful hands, pointed feet.
*"**Allosaurus** came to compete!"*
Her score makes her the one to beat.

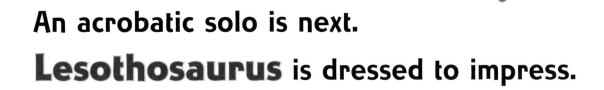

An acrobatic solo is next.

Lesothosaurus is dressed to impress.

The music is loud. His backflips are quick.

A straddle to split—what a neat trick!

Somersaults, walkovers, aerial twists—
He stands on one hand! *"It's all in the wrist!"*

Terrific technique! The crowd calls for more.
The judges concur. **Leso** gets the top score!

Who's the crew the crowd wants to see?
"The **Rhythmic Reds** from **TDC!**"

They strut onstage to a hip-hop sound,
pumped and ready to throw it down!

The **Reds** have attitude and swag.

"*We got this battle in the bag!*"

Front flips, toprock, isolations, headspins, K-kicks—

"*Complication!*"

BIG T-Rex says, *"Make some room!"*

Hits the floor with a *Boom! Boom! Boom!*

That B-boy's breakin'. 'Bout to get busy.

His windmill spins make dinos dizzy!

This hard-hitting hip-hop phenomenon
challenges green to "Bring it on!"

"Next up, Minmi's Dance Connection!"
Ready to rock and dressed to perfection.

They pump their fists and bend their knees,
then get down to the Green-Eyed Peas!

Here's **Triple T—Triceratops**.
He leads this crew in green high-tops.

At poppin' and lockin', he can't be caught.
'Cause he's the master of hip-hop.

He talks the talk. He walks the walk.
Watch him STOP . . .

. . . then drop it like it's hot!

Kentrosaurus

is all about jazz.

He dazzles the crowd

with style and pizzazz!

His smile is wide.

His graceful arms sweep.

Tombé to turn. Calypso leap!

He gives it his all and wants a good score.

Kentro drops to his knees and slides 'cross the floor.

The front row complains of a major mishap . . .

. . . as Kentro slides off into Diplo's wide lap!

Raptor and **Galli** take the stage
for a dance duet from a different age!

Trumpets blare and hepcats sing.
Jump and jive to a thing called swing!

Boogie-woogie, Charleston, Lindy Hop:
They dance through the decades.
"Will they never stop?!"

The crowd catches on to the swing-dance styles.
The audience and judges are boppin' in the aisles!

Maia and **Stego** step to the beat.

This duo is fluid, light on their feet.

To sizzle at salsa, you must move your hips.

There's shaking and shimmying, footwork and dips.

Feet fast as lightning! The two move as one.

Muy rápido dancing is part of the fun!

"Hey, folks, you ain't seen nothin' yet!"

The **Pterodactyls** perform a duet.

This tap-dance number takes place on the stairs.

Called "Me and My Shadow," it's perfect for pairs!

Ptero One starts with *tappity-tap*.

Ptero Two follows with *clackity-clack*.

Their footwork is flawless, their tapping, complex,
till **Ptero One's** shadow . . .

trips

down

the

steps!

The scores are all tallied, the judging complete.
Tricera is poised on the edge of his seat.

Leso takes solo! But we're not done yet.
Raptor and **Galli** win Swing Dance Duet!

But which team took hip-hop?
Just wait and see . . .

"The Rhythmic Red dancers from **Team TDC!**"

The competition season is done.
They spun, skipped, and swayed and had tons of fun.

What's next for the dancers? Without delay—
"Positions, please! There's no time to play!"

The Dinos make sport of the next holiday
and start to rehearse *The Nutcracker* ballet.
Because . . .

. . . Dino-Christmas is coming your way!